MW00949290

The Panda Who Would Not Eat

written and illustrated by
Ruth Todd Evans

Sunbelt Publications
San Diego, California

The Panda Who Would Not Eat

Copyright ©2008 by Ruth Todd Evans

Sunbelt Publications, Inc.
All rights reserved. First edition 2008
Edited by Jennifer Redmond
Book and cover design by Leah Cooper
Production Coordinator Jennifer Redmond
Printed in the United States of America by Walsworth

No part of this book may be reproduced in any form without permission
of the publisher. Please direct comments and inquiries to:

Sunbelt Publications, Inc.
P.O. Box 191126
San Diego, CA 92159-1126
(619) 258-4911, fax: (619) 258-4916
www.sunbeltbooks.com

12 11 10 09 08 07   5 4 3 2 1

Library of Congress Cataloging-in-Publication Data

Evans, Ruth Todd.
  The panda who would not eat / [written and illustrated by] Ruth Todd
Evans. -- 1st ed.
      p. cm.
  Summary: A panda that lives at the zoo stops eating until bamboo is
brought in from the botanical gardens. Based on a true story.
  ISBN-13: 978-0-932653-84-0
  ISBN-10: 0-932653-84-7
  [1. Pandas--Fiction. 2. Stories in rhyme.] I. Title.
  PZ8.3.E937Pan 2007
  [E]--dc22
                        2007030811

All illustrations by the author

Published in cooperation with...

and

Dedication

This book was conceived with Julie Mossy and Marilyn Herlihy Dronenburg. Julian Duval, CEO of **Quail Botanical Gardens**, related the true story of the panda at the **San Diego Zoo** who wanted to eat a variety of **Quail Botanical Gardens'** bamboo. We were enchanted by the tale and hope children and those reading the book to them will enjoy this fictionalized account of the story. We dedicate this book to our children and grandchildren.

Ruth Todd Evans has waived the royalties from this book as a gift to **Quail Botanical Gardens**.

A portion of the proceeds of this book will benefit the **Giant Panda Conservation** program and the new **Children's Garden** at **Quail Botanical Gardens**.

熊猫

There was a **panda**
who lived at the zoo

He was born in China
in a forest of bamboo

He ate and ate
bamboo at the zoo

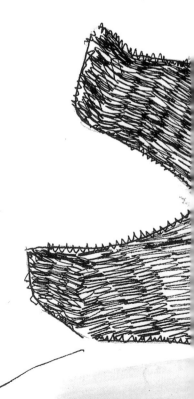

Until one day,
it is true...

He would not eat
the zoo bamboo!

熊猫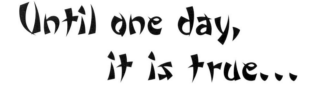

The keeper of the zoo
    wondered what to do

All pandas
    eat bamboo!!!

The children thought
of a cake
with bamboo

熊猫

Or a **lollipop** or two...

熊
猫

But pandas just
eat bamboo...

熊猫

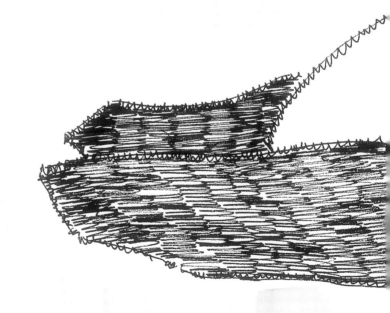

"Quail Botanical Gardens
has lots of bamboo"
said the keeper at the zoo

"Will this panda eat
a new bamboo?"

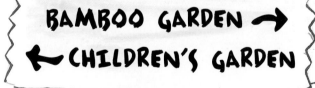

BAMBOO GARDEN →
← CHILDREN'S GARDEN

QUAIL
BOTANICAL GARDENS

熊猫

"Could the truck from the zoo
come for the Gardens' bamboo?"

熊猫

"Yes,"
   said the staff at the Gardens,
      "please do!"

The truck with the special bamboo
arrived back at the zoo

and the panda ate
the new bamboo!!

熊
猫

The panda kept eating
at the zoo...

Trucks kept bringing
more truckloads too

Now that the panda
WOULD EAT
the bamboo!!

Author's Notes

The Real Panda Who Wouldn't Eat was Shi Shi, the first male panda in the San Diego Zoo Giant Panda Conservation program. He was a picky eater and really wanted to eat one species of bamboo from Quail Botanical Gardens in San Diego County. Shi-Shi has returned to China and lives at the Woolong Nature Preserve. Zoo trucks still go to Quail Botanical Gardens for some of the bamboo for the pandas.

The Panda is the symbol of the World Wildlife Federation. There are believed to be 1600 pandas in the world at this time. Giant Panda Conservation programs like those at the San Diego Zoo are helping to prevent these bears from becoming extinct. The panda is one of the symbols of the 2008 Summer Olympic Games in China.

Bamboo provides 99% of the pandas' diet. The world famous San Diego Zoo grows 67 species of bamboo. Quail Botanical Gardens is a 35-acre botanical garden in Encinitas in San Diego County. It has 120 species of bamboo—more species than any other botanical garden in North America.

The Calligraphy on each page is the word "panda" in Chinese. The symbols stand for "bear" and "cat."

The Chinese Seal on each page means "for our descendents." Both the San Diego Zoo and Quail Botanical Gardens are striving to save plants and animals for our descendents. They both provide children with a haven dedicated to learning experiences about plants and animals and the world of nature around them.